D1311847

9

MOONBEAR'S PET

A MOONBEAR Book

· FRANK ASCH ·

ALADDIN

NEW YORK   LONDON   TORONTO   SYDNEY   NEW DELHI

ALADDIN

An imprint of Simon & Schuster Children's Publishing Division

1230 Avenue of the Americas, New York, NY 10020

This Aladdin edition August 2014

For information about special discounts for bulk purchases, please contact Simon & Schuster Special Sales at 1-866-506-1949 or business@simonandschuster.com.

The Simon & Schuster Speakers Bureau can bring authors to your live event. For more information or to book an event contact the Simon & Schuster Speakers Bureau at 1-866-248-3049 or visit our website at www.simonspeakers.com.

Designed by Karina Granda

The text of this book was set in Olympian LT Std.

The illustrations for this book were rendered digitally.

Manufactured in China 0614 SCP

10 9 8 7 6 5 4 3 2 1

Library of Congress Cataloging-in-Publication Data

Asch, Frank

Moonbear's pet / Frank Asch.

p. cm.

Summary: Bear and Little Bird find a baby fish in their pond and decide to keep her for a pet, but when she starts to sprout wings, or maybe paws, each thinks the fish wants to be like him, which puts a strain on their friendship.

[1. Bears—Fiction. 2. Birds—Fiction. 3. Tadpoles—Fiction. 4. Friendship—Fiction.] I. Title.

PZ7.A778Bf 1997

[E]—dc20 95-30011

ISBN 978-1-4424-9429-9 (pbk)

ISBN 978-1-4424-9430-5 (hc)

ISBN 978-1-4424-9431-2 (eBook)

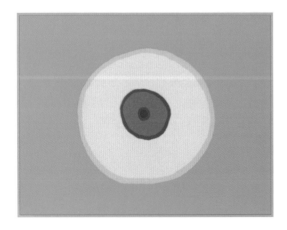

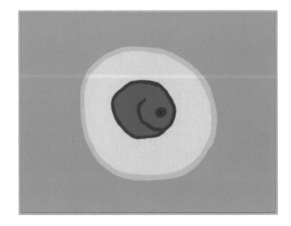

To Sarah and Caitlin

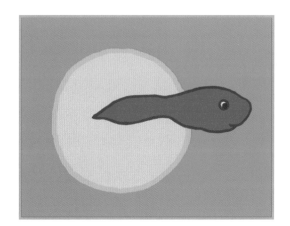

One spring day while playing in the pond, Bear found a new pet.

"Oh, what a cute little fishy!" cried his friend Little Bird. "What will you call her?"

As Bear hurried home, he thought of names like Skinny, Sweetpea, and Slowpoke. But none of those names seemed quite right.

Then he dropped his pet into a bowl of water, and she landed with a *splash*.

"That's it!" cried Bear. "We'll call her Splash!"

Bear and Little Bird loved to watch Splash swim and blow bubbles.

They put Splash on the floor while they played and on the kitchen table while they ate.

After lunch they took Splash outside to watch while they worked in Bear's garden.

They even took Splash shopping!

Every night after Little Bird flew home to his nest, Bear stayed up late talking to Splash and telling her bedtime stories.

Every morning Little Bird brought Splash a present: an acorn, a seashell, a pretty pebble, or a pink button.

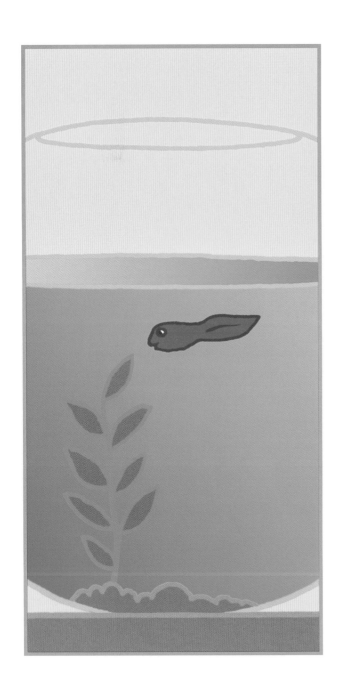

As the days and weeks passed

Splash grew bigger and bigger.

One day Little Bird chirped, "Look! Splash is growing wings. She must want to be a bird just like me!"

Bear took a close look at Splash. "Those aren't wings. See! There are four of them. They must be paws. Splash is becoming a bear just like me!"

"Why would anyone want to be a clumsy old bear when they can be a beautiful bird?" chirped Little Bird.

"Indeed!" exclaimed Bear. "Why would anyone want to be a chirpy sack of feathers when they could be a big strong bear?"

"Well, I guess we'll just have to let Splash decide for herself!" huffed Little Bird.

"That's just fine with me!" Bear huffed back.

So Bear and Little Bird put Splash in a tiny pool next to
Bear's pond and promised each other not to visit her for
a month.

"And don't visit me, either!" said Bear.

"I wouldn't dream of it!" snapped Little Bird.

Bear and Little Bird used to play together.

Now they played alone.

At the end of the month Bear and Little Bird met at Splash's pool.

"Now we'll see what a fine bear she's become," mumbled Bear.

"Or what a fine bird," grumbled Little Bird.

But Splash wasn't in the pool.

"Splash!" Little Bird called up to the sky.

"Splash!" Bear called into the woods.

Just then a young frog hopped up and croaked, "Here I am!"

"Please don't bother us now, little frog," said Bear. "We're looking for my pet, Splash!"

"But I'm Splash," said the frog.

"But you're not a bear!" said Bear.

"Or a bird!" said Little Bird.

"I was never a fish, either," said Splash." I was a tadpole. And tadpoles don't become bears or birds. They become frogs!"

Bear was so surprised! All he could say was, "But wouldn't you rather be a bear?"

"I'd rather be a frog," said Splash.

"But wouldn't it be best if we were all birds?" said Little Bird.

"No," replied Splash calmly. "I think it would be best if we were all friends."

Bear was silent for a moment. Then he said "I think she's right."

"I agree," sighed Little Bird.

"I missed you, Little Bird," whispered Bear.

"I missed you, too," Little Bird whispered back.

"And I missed both of you," cried Splash. "Come on! Let's all go for a swim!"

"Good idea!" said Bear.

"Great idea!" chirped Little Bird.

And they all jumped into the pond with a splash!